STOMPIN' TOM CONNORS

HOCKEY
NIGHT TONIGHT
THE HOCKEY SONG

RAGWEED
THE ISLAND PUBLISHER

ILLUSTRATIONS BY BRENDA JONES

10   9   8   7   6   5   4   3   2   1

The song "The Hockey Song" performed by Stompin' Tom Connors is available
from EMI Music Canada on the following albums:
Stompin' Tom And The Hockey Song C2-93049
Once Upon A Stompin' Tom C2-97103
Kic* Along With Stompin' Tom S2-89451
*(Keep It Canadian)

Ragweed Press acknowledges the support of the Canada Council.

The publisher wishes to thank the Toronto Maple Leafs and the
Montreal Canadiens for kind permission to use their team logos.

Printed and bound in Hong Kong by:
Wing King Tong

Published by:
Ragweed Press
P.O. Box 2023
Charlottetown, P.E.I.
Canada C1A 7N7

Canadian Cataloguing in Publication Data

Connors, Stompin' Tom, 1936-

Hockey night tonight

ISBN 0-921556-57-8

I. Jones, Brenda, 1953- II. Title.

PS8555.05577H63 1995   jC811.'54   C95-950141-X
PZ8.3.C66Ho 1995

Hello out there, we're on the air,

It's hockey night tonight!

Tension grows, the whistle blows,

And the puck goes down the ice;

The goalie jumps, the players bump,

And the fans all go insane;

Someone roars, Bobby scores,

At the good old hockey game.

Oh, the good old hockey game

Is the best game you can name;

And the best game you can name

Is the good old hockey game.

Where players dash with skates aflash,

The home team trails behind;

But they grab the puck and go bursting up,

And they're down across the line;

They storm the crease like bumble bees,

They travel like a burning flame;

We see them slide the puck inside —

It's a one – one hockey game!

Oh, the good old hockey game

Is the best game you can name;

And the best game you can name

Is the good old hockey game.

Third period, last game in the playoffs, too...

Oh, take me where the hockey players
Face off down the rink;

And the Stanley Cup is all filled up

For the champs who win the drink;

Now the final flick of a hockey stick,
And one gigantic scream;
The puck is in, the home team wins
The good old hockey game.

Oh, the good old hockey game

Is the best game you can name;

And the best game you can name

Is the good old hockey game.

Hello out there, we're on the air,
It's hockey night tonight!
Tension grows, the whistle blows,
And the puck goes down the ice;
The goalie jumps, the players bump,
And the fans all go insane;
Someone roars, Bobby scores,
At the good old hockey game.

Oh, the good old hockey game
Is the best game you can name;
And the best game you can name
Is the good old hockey game.

Second period...
Where players dash with skates aflash,
The home team trails behind;
But they grab the puck and go bursting u
And they're down across the line;
They storm the crease like bumble bees,
They travel like a burning flame;
We see them slide the puck inside —
It's a one – one hockey game!

Oh, the good old hockey game
Is the best game you can name;
And the best game you can name
Is the good old hockey game.

Third period, last game in the playoffs, too...
Oh, take me where the hockey players
Face off down the rink;
And the Stanley Cup is all filled up
For the champs who win the drink;
Now the final flick of a hockey stick,
And one gigantic scream;
The puck is in, the home team wins
The good old hockey game.

Oh, the good old hockey game
Is the best game you can name;
And the best game you can name
Is the good old hockey game.